Renier-Fréduman Mundil

Allegories

Volume 2
Short Stories

Renier-Fréduman Mundil

Allegories

Volume 2
Short Stories

Translated from German
by Hilary Teske

Bibliographic information from the German National Library:
The German National Library lists this publication in the
German National Bibliography; detailed bibliographic data is
available online at http://dnb.dnb.de.

Cover design: Dan Winkler
Editing: Malin Friese
Publisher: BoD · Books on Demand GmbH,
Überseering 33, 22297 Hamburg, bod@bod.de
Print: Libri Plureos GmbH, Friedensallee 273,
22763 Hamburg

ISBN: 978-3-8192-8015-3

For
Sophie

Introduction

The allegory is a linguistic placeholder for the parable. To understand a person better, it is worth looking at their whole family. The family member parable has many relatives, obviously close relatives such as mother, father, brother and sister as well as those who have married in from some distant side, adopted, there are also first cousins (first degree) as well as untraceable 25th cousins (25th degree) and probably also a number of family members who are not such – those who simply went to the wedding party, although they had no connection to the family, but pretended to be a deeply connected family member.

A colourful mixture of kinship called allegory, analogy, comparison, simile, didactic piece, metaphor, allegory, similitude, maschal and nimschal and others.

As this picture is very colourful, we can easily imagine that parables not only play a role in the Jewish or Christian religion, but also in many other religions, cultures and poems.

The undisputed grandmaster of the parable is Jesus Christ. He is said to have told (sorry, I haven't counted) 48 parables in the New Testament.

The following is an extract:

- The fig tree (with and without fruit)
- Creditor and two debtors
- House built on rock and sand
- The guest without a wedding garment
- The wise and foolish virgins
- The pearl of great price
- The camel and the eye of the needle
- New wine in old wineskins
- The leavened bread
- The unmerciful creditor
- Treasure in the field
- Mustard seed
- Entrusted talents
- Tares and wheat
- The Last Judgement
- The unjust judge
- The prodigal son
- The lost sheep
- The lost coin
- The Good Samaritan
- The sower

Although Christ used everyday life at that time for his parables - for example, there were no street lamps, everyone walked with an oil lamp, the seed was not sown with millimetre precision using a machine but was scattered by hand, seeds fell on stones, under weeds, etc. - although he used these situations, which we rarely encounter in our everyday lives, they still leave a deep impression today. They are easy to remember with a hidden important message that we discover when we think about them.

One of the things that impressed me was the parable of the five wise and five foolish virgins. All ten waited for the Lord, who did not come at the expected time. When he appeared, the oil lamps were empty. The five wise virgins had a reserve, refilled their lamps and were invited to the wedding feast in heaven. The five foolish ones first had to go to the city to refill their lamps. When they stood at the gates of heaven, these were and remained closed. They were too late, a moment too late because of their negligence, and this brief moment meant that they had to stand outside the locked gates of heaven for an eternity.

This parable reminded me of an incident with my father. We were repairing the drain in the kitchen at home and realised just before we finished that a piece was missing. So we rushed off, ran to the underground, travelled seven stops and rushed to the nearest plumbing shop. Back then, there were no large, almost permanently open DIY shops, and there was no such thing as same-day express delivery via the internet. None of that existed yet.

We arrived at the small shop at exactly 1.01 pm, 1 minute after closing time. Behind the glass pane, we saw the owner locking the door at various levels. We were able to talk to him through the glass door, complaining about our misery, a weekend without normal drainage of the dishwater, no, we would have to dispose of each bowl separately. None of it helped. The owner would not budge. We were standing in front of a closed toilet cubicle for a minute.

That day, there wasn't another young person in the world who understood the five foolish virgins better than I did.

Parables come to life when we look at them through our everyday lives, even if they look different (but only outwardly) from the time of Christ.

The German word Geglichenes (here translated as allegory) also has relatives: Ausgeglichenes (balance), Abgeglichenes (alignment), Beglichenes (settlement), Verglichenes (comparison) and certainly even more relatives. If we join each of these different family members and look at the parable from the different positions, then a rounded picture emerges from everything, which is what we often strive for in life.

In every parable there is an equation made up of a number of unknowns.

> 1. OT + NT = BB or
> 2. OT + NT = L

The first equation is simple:

OT (Old Testament) + **NT** (New Testament) = **BiBle**.

But the second equation has another explanation. OT is not only the **Old Testament** but also **Ordinary Times**.

O(rdinary)T(imes) + N(ew) T(estament) = Life.

That is the equation behind the parables: the ordinary times links up with the New Testament or the parables so abundant there and results in

(=) life. And which of us doesn't like to understand our complicated lives through this simple equation?

The following collection contains just over 60 short stories, each of which is based on a biblical passage, usually from the New Testament. As we have four children, the stories are deliberately divided into four volumes, a small legacy to the children to discover in their own lives or the lives of their own families the precious treasure of the parables that Christ so often used. A short time to catch your breath, a short time perhaps to reflect, a short time perhaps to delve deeper.

1.
Accompanied alone

Darkness. Blackness. The trees dead. Not a leaf moved. Dead branches, death clung to them. The nearby hills cast great shadows on the landscape. The sun ducked behind them. Blazing red, almost black, it dipped into the line of the horizon. Mosquitos flickered in its parting light, circling each other, making buzzing sounds in the air before dissolving into nothingness.

The light went out in the houses. Eyelids fell shut. Over the cares of the day. Covered in the hardship of everyday life. Roughened feet lay motionless under torn out feathers. Stale air flowed out of the sleeping bodies. The dogs lay in the kitchen, the cold evening air creeping out of the floor, entangling itself in their fur.

Outside, two figures were walking through the evening. Their eyes were turned forward, but their thoughts were turned towards each other. They couldn't understand what had happened. From time to time, their voices became agitated, then fell back into the monotony of resignation. What was happening was unimaginable. The voices flickered once more, more violently than before. Reproaches resounded, the night covered the expressions on their faces.

Then they walked side by side in silence. Through the night. To escape the darkness. To find refuge in a building. To sit in the light of a lamp. To clear their thoughts. Speech has died out, the flow of words has dried up, the feet are just rolling along.

It was bound to happen. Don't you understand?

They walked on. A cool wind blew out of the forest and gave them new strength. The muscles in their feet contracted faster. The dry branches crackled under their feet.

What is this event you are talking about?

The sound of their voices became more familiar. They were no strangers in the big city. Everyone had noticed. The locals, travelers, guests, the rich and the beggars, even the blind and the deaf had not been unaware.

I'm the only one who didn't find out. What were your thoughts agitated about? What takes the sound of your words and adapts it to the gloomy evening atmosphere?

It was three days ago. Our hopes were pinned on him and he carried the burden of expectation.

We thought so. Until they arrested him. No, it was different. He allowed himself to be arrested. Certainly, he could have fled. He had followers everywhere. Many would have hidden him. No, not many. Well, not many, but enough to escape the henchmen. Dungeons instead. Thick walls. No liberation. Not for us. Not for him. Until he disappeared. Suddenly. If it was true. Women wanted to visit him. Bring him fresh food and comfort. His cell was empty. The guards kept silent about his whereabouts. It was three days ago. The women's visit.

The night had grown darker. Black leaves and the black horizon merged into a wall, no beginning, no end. The contours of their discouraged faces were lost in the darkness. Their empty hearts sucked in great draughts of the black night, no solace anywhere, no hope, their leader had disappeared, with him their dreams, painstakingly nurtured expectations, almost exhausted patience.

You should understand, it was for the best. His disappearance will give the others courage. He has gone to be much closer to you. You used to be able to see him, now you can feel him, the power of memory. Feeling is closer than seeing,

seeing and remembering, both perhaps equally distant. It was predicted – by many people in the movement. Only most of them didn't want to believe. Neither do you two. You only need to read speech of the old ones carefully, the path was mapped out, one step, the next step, to the end. If he had stayed, you would not have remembered him.

The two of them gazed into the dark evening. You hadn't remembered. Of course, he had to go to be with them. Why hadn't they understood before? Their thoughts flared up. The meaning of his disappearance, the prison, it was empty, at least the women, they had reported it, everything added up to a meaning that erased the dark thoughts, hopelessness, resignation, profound disappointment, incomprehension.

A warm feeling spread out. It was dark outside. The night had fallen. The horizon was black. The forest was black. The leaves motionless, dead branches, life had vanished behind cold walls.

How foolish you are, and how slow to believe all that the prophets have spoken! (Luke 24:25)

As they approached the village to which they were going, Jesus continued on as if he were going farther. But they urged him strongly, Stay with us, for it is nearly evening; the day is almost over. (Luke 24:28,29)

2.
Artificial Babel-like height

The wood was more polished than the glittering steel construction of the façade. A thick piece of lush wood, cut from the trunk of a giant tree in the primeval forest. From it a tabletop, in the shape of the land. Up here, on the 102nd floor, the precious wood was enthroned much higher than it would ever have been allowed to as part of the sequoia tree. Up here, not a leaf flew past the window, not a bird, not a bee, the only life consisted of people. 15 of them sat around this thick, shiny fillet of wood. The atmosphere was tense, the old wood fibers calmed the nerves.

It is impossible to raise it again.
To the left, at the coastal seat of the map-like wooden table, one of the men had spoken up.

Believe me, it's impossible. No one will tolerate it.
Head shaking, first from the chairman, when the others saw it, their heads shook too. The direction suddenly became clear.

They've said it every time, the chairman turned to the speaker. At least for the last seven prize rounds. If we had listened to them,

I don't want to know, I don't want to know, I don't want to....

Those present watched him intently. Something unexpected had happened. Or so they thought. But only the secretary of the supervisory board had entered. But that could mean a lot of things. The meeting could only be disturbed in an extreme emergency. She walked straight to the chairman, her endless legs disappearing far too soon behind her blue skirt. She walked at a good pace, her black hair flying to the side, a breeze rushing through the room.

Wordlessly, she handed over a fax. She did a pirouette on her stiletto heels, got tangled up, fell forward, just managed to regain her balance and disappeared under the dripping gazes of the men.

They had time to stare after the legs that had disappeared too soon, the chairman took some time to study the document.

Let's continue, gentlemen, he finally said and turned his back to the wall again, or to put it more simply, he turned back to those present.

Let us continue, he repeated, I ask for further comments.

These came. Their essence was clear. Given by the chairman's head shake. The score was 14:1, a result that corresponded to the corner ratio of an uneven soccer match.

Nevertheless, it seemed important to the chairman to continue working on the dissenting vote.

You're right, Winston. Our camps are full. But how quickly that can change. We also have to think about the war chest, takeovers are imminent, so we need a little change in the petty cash. And your salary, Winston. You know as well as I do that it depends on the share price. And that depends on our profits. And it climbs with the price per liter. We'll raise it by two cents. Every month. On average. Interrupted by the usual ups and downs. There's no hardship, but do we have to get to the point where we're talking about hardship? Two cents a month. Not the father of the family. Not the cab driver. You know as well as I do, Winston, the law stakes out the marketplace, and someone has to lay down the law. The others will see it as unfair anyway, no matter what they do.

I'm meeting with the chairmen of the other companies tomorrow. Gentlemen, I am pleased to be able to tell the others tomorrow that we will continue to toe the line we have agreed together.

It was easy, Winston thought. Yellow, blue, green, red, they all followed the agreed path, an average of two cents a month, interrupted by ups and downs, albeit at different rates, sometimes the reds went up and the greens down, one week the greens went up sharply, the reds stayed put, now the yellows joined in, slowly climbing higher.

Everything was meticulously planned by a random generator, only the goal was fixed, a summit, 2 meters higher, where everyone would meet after 30 days. A place by the yellow sun, which had risen red, smiling down on the green land in the blue sky. Not for the many small black dots of people scurrying across the land. For the large structures. They were the ones who had hoisted the magnificent wooden fillet from the nothingness of a jungle tree, between darkness, ferns, lianas and stuffy air, to a height of 400 meters.

Winston stood up. What advice. Another unjust decision.

The chairman tried to hold him.

Wait a minute, Winston. This fax is from the President. He's congratulating us on last year's profits. And look Winston, he writes that he needs money, people will be pumping less, so what, the higher price will bring in more taxes. You see Winston.
He didn't look. He didn't look. Wrongly, perhaps.
Now there was a man named Joseph, a member of the Council, a good and upright man, who had not consented to their decision and action because it was wrong.
(Luke 23: 50-51)

3.

Involuntary natural turnaround

Bryan Edward Arthur Smith. Actually, he had even more first names. Bryan Edward Arthur, they were the names of his ancestors, grandfather, great-uncle, great-great-grandfather. These three were the most athletic from a long family line of top athletes, which is why he had been given these names, with them the sporting heritage had been laid in his cradle.

His parents were crazy, in a positive sense, to assume something special just by looking at him. When he was still a baby, they observed the rocking of the cradle when he moved, and it seemed to them that none of the other children had made their presence felt as powerfully through the swinging of the cradle. His first attempt at crawling was compared to the movements of a Greco-Roman freestyle wrestler, who also crawled across the floor, staring at his opponent.

Perhaps this was his destiny.

The first steps caused an enthusiastic chain of excitement in the family, powerful, energetic, like a grizzly, yet supple, like a wildcat, they surpassed the movements of the most famous football players. At the age of three, he rode his bike perfectly and the professionals didn't have a better posture on their bikes. If, yes, if it wasn't for his powerful way of plowing through the water with his arms. Of course, he was the fastest in his year at high school. Swimming also accelerated his growth. He was 10 cm short of the height of a basketball player. 10 cm, he would make it too. Size paired with marksmanship, the high school teams were already clamoring for him – Bryan Arthur Edward, everything had come together for him.

And overflowed. Like being in a too small barrel, caught in a downpour.

The proportions were no longer right. Suddenly he looked more like a basketball player in the water, his football game resembled that of a professional cyclist without a bicycle. There were huge snags everywhere, he was tangled up in invisible chains, chains, not ropes, not a Gordian knot that could be cut with a single stroke.

A long time ago. 30 years? 40 years? Many years. Old age, bloated flesh, brittle bones, immobile joints, cloudy eyes, the snails in his ears no longer able to perceive the approach of an opponent in time. The complex stretched endlessly. Gray walls, interspersed with openings, windows, small, set straight as a die, morning admission for the day, evening gateway to the night. Behind every window a room, small, cage-like, bed, table, chair, telephone, access to a bathroom, square chamber, then a shower area, at ground level, toilet, handbasin, opening for the air conditioning, in whose wake the lives of the old people disappeared.

Bryan Edward Arthur, decades ago you were a man, young, muscles everywhere, tendons fixed to iron-firm bones, incredible responsiveness, wide awake, multi-talented, high school girls' crush, now, years, decades swallowed up, body lying on a bed, lying in the morning, lying in the evening, lying in between, no longer able to get up on your own, plowing through the water, chasing balls, tensing muscles, not seeing who was at the door. When someone came, your ear heard nothing.

Very truly I tell you, when you were younger you dressed yourself and went where you wanted; but when you are old you will stretch out your hands, and someone else will dress you and lead you where you do not want to go. (John 21:18)

4.

The avowed slander

I will never forget that day. It's amazing how seemingly trivial things in life never leave your mind, while important events are erased from your memory a few years later. Never forget. It's strange, I remember something that never happened. We're better at remembering events that never happened anyway. Reproach, conscience, disappointment, everything keeps these things that never happened alive. A lot is built on this principle, including hell, if you believe some views on it.

Remembering something that never happened. A lesson. Even then, many lessons were canceled. This one was also canceled. Nevertheless, we had to stay in the classroom, the lesson was canceled and never took place. To make sure we stayed, we were assigned a supervisor. Two girls from an older class, model pupils, were, I found out later, absolutely loyal to the school.

However, they didn't give any substitute lessons but played a stupid game with us. Until I suddenly realized that, from my point of view at the time, I was heading for disaster. An interrogation game. A statistic. A socio-demographic survey. They asked how many siblings everyone had. What was the most common family size? And, I saw a razor-sharp cliff emerging from the sea, there was no way around it. Maybe with a ship called Nausea, but even then it was reserved for girls. Who had the most siblings. I knew about my lonely top position. I would hardly be presented with a trophy for that. At most a bucket of all possible contempt.

When I was asked for seven siblings – I was sweating blood and water at the time – the bell rang. I will never forget the sound of the school bell. I was no longer at the age when I realized the social consequences of a large family, and not yet in those years when people proudly pointed out this peculiarity in a biography. Back then, I was deep in the mire of worrying endlessly – even unnecessarily – about what my classmates might think about this or that aspect of my social background.

I was still in the same period of my life when a similar situation happened to me in my French lessons. With a teacher. I was something like her favorite because, although I was a boy, I was the best at French. Languages were the domain of girls, but here I was the top dog. And we were supposed to express in French how many brothers we had. The line of answers moved inexorably towards me, I feverishly calculated how many brothers I had, they first had to be separated from the girls like black goats from white ones.

I was amazed, nine, there were nine brothers. I saw everything collapse. The approval of my teacher, the admiration of the girls, at that time and at that age, one was not loved for having nine brothers. The ship called Nausea appeared, it was already full of girls, I could no longer escape with it. Une frère, I thought, and frère might sound a bit similar to neuf, I'll mumble une frère, so I pulled my head out of the noose.

Which was nonsense of course, brothers always remain masculine, so of course it had to be un frère. My French teacher also interpreted this from my answer. She just shook her head. What a stupid mistake, from her best pupil, it's not une frère but un frère, she corrected in horror. I stuck with une, after all, the truth, the nine, the neuf, should resonate somewhere in my answer.

I had grown a little older and was a little more susceptible to the feeling of doing wrong, I had denied my family. Perhaps a few people understand me, not because they have a similar number of siblings, perhaps they have traveled a similar path to be able to speak freely about the fact that there is an alcoholic, a criminal, someone infected with AIDS, the list could go on and on, in their family.

I was ashamed at first, but life is fair, there are still opportunities later. Like now. I am proud of my family, my parents, and I am not ashamed of them, I love them, they gave life to 13 children, ten boys and three girls, and took on more than I did in two lousy lessons.

When they had finished eating, Jesus said to Simon Peter, Simon son of John, do you love me more than these?

Yes, Lord, he said, You know that I love you.

(John 21:15)

Looking back on my time in history, I think I should be proud of my family more than once, I have told you about two incidents, how many have I forgotten?

The third time he said to him, Simon son of John, do you love me? (John 21:17).

5.
Hunger in disguise

It was terrible in the city, beggars, homeless people, almost every corner had someone sitting quietly immersed in themselves, a lifeless hand outstretched. But that was not enough. They sent children on tour. You could perhaps resist the old, neglected, emaciated bodies. But these children? Huge, expectant eyes, fragile hands reaching out towards you. Only the imagination helped. Usually came of its own accord. Somewhere there was a patron, a clan chief, who had trained the little ones to beg, if not to steal, and not five minutes later the coin would end up in the hands of a disgusting guy. This idea helped to keep the wallet closed even in front of small, wide eyes and fragile, tiny fingers.

Anyway, the taxes. You had to pay more taxes every week. If you weren't a beggar yourself, a beggar in your own country, and then these dark-skinned strangers came and sent their children – they were probably too cowardly to beg by themselves. Feeling sorry for yourself also helped to keep your wallet closed. Over time, people learned the tricks of not succumbing to the danger of their own good nature.

Over time, a subconscious mood built up in him without him realizing it. He no longer looked, if he passed a beggar or was approached by one. The misery of others had become something normal, like the weather, the trees, the cars on the street. It was part of the colorful picture of life, you would even miss it if there was no hardship, how dreary your own life would be if these splashes of color were missing.

It was only one stage of the subconscious development, the process was slowly progressing. Now the beggars began to bother him. Did they have to sit in front of the entrance to the department store of all places, nobody could get into the store comfortably anymore, everything was cramped and crowded anyway and the little bit of warm air could be found elsewhere. Why did the beggar stretch out his feet on the street, couldn't he imagine that others would stumble along, faithfully following their daily routine? The barrel overflowed as the beggars pursued him. They no longer stayed in the city, but began to walk through the suburbs, ringing doorbells and garden doorbells, disturbing the well-earned peace at home.

When the bell rang, he saw the young man at the garden gate. He had forgotten exactly what he said, but the man had disappeared before he could repeat his begging request.

He returned to the house without a thought.

Who was at the door?

Oh, some beggar.

What did he want?

I don't know.

Did you give him anything?

No, why should I?

You should have at least offered him a sandwich. Maybe he was hungry.

Hungry? It hadn't occurred to him at all. Maybe it wasn't someone who had his car around the corner, maybe he was just hungry, hadn't had anything to eat for several days, just wanted to satisfy the black hunger in his stomach. Simply eat something.

Early in the morning, Jesus stood on the shore, but the disciples did not realize that it was Jesus. He called out to them, Friends, haven't you any fish? No, they answered.
(John 21:4-5)

6.

The incredible normality

How many people, masses, countless, many, but how many? People everywhere, to his left, in front of him, behind him, simply everywhere. Jubilee. City celebration. The city had turned 750 years old. Everything must be celebrated. Who knows how long there will be something to celebrate. The fireworks were huge. Not loud, soft colors, the firmament, the simple clear beauty of the starry sky faded against this impression. What is close to us is big, but what is small in the distance is what is truly important. In the distance. So much lay there. An endless graveyard of memories, lined up next to each other, polished crosses for buried hopes, thousands of massacred expectations, blood-soaked, deeply scarred faces next to them, involved next to uninvolved, laughing, sad, a blueprint of life.

The fireworks were still crackling. The moon had raised a thick blanket of clouds, it seemed too much for the old man, noise, flashes of light, people shouting. The cloud formations were more interesting than the symmetrical, sterile images of lights, night formations, born of the imagination, searching for their image, inexhaustible like the constant sound of waves, the flame of fire, always the same, yet different at every moment.

When he closed his eyes, the beacons appeared between his eyes and eyelids, pale, flickering gnats, from there they disappeared into the convolutions of his brain. When he opened his eyes, it took countless moments for him to realize it.

His best friend was standing in front of him. No, it wasn't his best friend. A friend, yes, even his best friend. But he wasn't standing in front of him, couldn't be standing in front of him. Ever. He wasn't in any other country. He wasn't on the other side of the world, didn't live in another city. He was simply dead. Everyone had received the message, black on white, the black cross of the dead on the pure white paper, his friend's name underneath, fragile letters dissolving on the pale paper.

No one had been able to grasp it. Him least of all. He had even written to the relevant authorities and had received documentary confirmation of the name, date of death, place, time, and location of the grave. Of course he had gone there. To the cemetery. A simple site, after he had left behind the magnificent rows of trees on the main path. Narrow graves, lined up next to each other, with the headstone at the top where the head rested.

Just as simple, one word: "Goodbye".

He recognized the gravestone immediately, a boulder split in two, it used to stand in his friend's garden. Where was the other half? Death, too, is made up of two halves, opposites, grief and... Death had passed, the second half of death stood before him.

His friend noticed his astonishment.

I'm not a ghost, he said, reaching into his bag of potato chips as confirmation and eating some of the crunchy pieces.

I told you, he heard the friend's voice, close and at the same time far away, from another world, I'm coming back to meet you again.

One more time? You, the others. Of course, it flashed through his mind. He had to tell the others immediately. He grabbed his friend and dragged him out of the crowd.

You have to tell me everything, tell us everything, he corrected himself. Everyone thought you were dead. And now, now you're standing here. Everyone thought you were dead, he repeated incredulously.

I was dead, the friend replied.
There was a warm tone to his voice that he couldn't quite put his finger on. There was certainty behind the words, joy, knowledge before the great task of making it plausible to his brain and now to the others, an infinite number of tones mixed into his words.
He could no longer hear it. He looked skeptically at his friend who had emerged from death, from a safe distance, and made a cell phone call to a comrade. His voice cracked as he relayed the message.
The other end of the line went dead silent, then the other person's voice answered:
'I don't believe you. Not until I've seen it for myself. It's impossible, I have to see it for myself. Do you remember our adventures? Back at camp, he tripped and fell into the camp fire. He has burn marks on both palms. Let me show you the scars. I want to see them too. I won't believe it until I've seen the scars. Only then.

Now Thomas (also known as Didymus), one of the Twelve, was not with the disciples when Jesus came. So the other disciples told him, We have seen the Lord!

But he said to them, Unless I see the nail marks in his hands and put my finger where the nails were, and put my hand into his side, I will not believe. (John 20:24-25)

7.

Too many too few baskets

Nothing is impossible. Can this sentence actually be uttered without immediately mentioning the brand name of a car? Many things are impossible. At times, everything seems to be, at least when chain after chain of failures are lined up.

The whole book was full of the impossible. The woman had been suffering from bleeding for years. No one could help. For twelve years. Others were helped by this problem. Had been treated by many doctors. The result: she suffered greatly. Her entire fortune was used up (but it had certainly helped the doctors). But that was not enough. Her condition had become even worse. This was not the first time that medical treatment had led to this unfortunate triad.

And where the doctors' art had failed, was touching the hem of his robe supposed to have helped? Many things are impossible. Likewise, to heal ten lepers with a miracle. No, that is not impossible. Something else. Healing ten people and thinking that everyone would be grateful. They've forgotten you faster than you've gotten to know them. You're lucky they didn't come back to reproach you for why you let them suffer, why they weren't healed sooner, why they were only healed and didn't receive a good package of other blessings at the same time – as compensation, so to speak. It's unbelievable to receive gratitude from everyone just because you helped them. Is that why you shouldn't help them? Perhaps only if you are after their gratitude. That can be a rude awakening for the helper.

Becoming like the children. Impossible. Unless someone remains a child throughout and never lets this mantle be torn off. Wouldn't be necessary if everyone became like children. 10% would be enough. 10% of all adults, in their attitude and non-attitude, their spontaneity and lack of prejudice, would be enough to put a big smiley face on this whole world. Impossible, it has already been established.

It's easier to take a dead boy from Nain by the hand and drag him back to life. You just have to pull at the right moment, with the right force and in the right direction. Not easy. Who has ever tried to put a dead, stiff body on its feet without it toppling over again? It's all a question of balance. Difficult and yet easier than many things.

You would need 200 denarii and a baker nearby. That would be enough to feed an evening party of 5,000 guests, provided they weren't too demanding. That's 0.04 denarii per person. Not a bad effort to get some gratitude in return. Where was there a baker in the desert? Nowhere. But there were two fish. Two fish in the desert. How did the fish get into the desert? And five loaves of bread must have grown on trees, like the sweet manna in the days of the ancient fathers. That made 0.0004 fish and 0.001 loaves per guest. Not a bad average compared to people who starve because they have less. You could give them the twelve baskets left over. Nothing is impossible.

How many loaves fit into twelve baskets? Certainly, more than five. What kind of fish were they? Whale fish? Perhaps one of the 5000 guests happened to have two whales with him. There have always been exotic fish. Two whale fish were enough to feed more than 5000 people. And the bread? Perhaps a giant had lost them, Gulliver or a giant from the land of Canaan, hadn't the ancients written about giants in the

Promised Land? Or perhaps an exotic person. Wanted to get into the Guinness Book with the loaves. Let's say each loaf was 1 m high, 15 m long and 3 m wide. That's why they didn't need chairs. They just sat down on the loaves. Nibbled their way into the pleasant shape of a chair, then continued to listen to the message.

Nothing is impossible, even with bread. Become like the children. If you give them fresh bread, it's gone in a flash. But with stale bread, they are already full at the sight of it. Perhaps the 5000 had already become like children. Just a crumb was enough, for various reasons, perhaps because it was an old crumb, to fill them up.

Five loaves and two fish – it turned out to be far too much. Invite 5000 guests but be careful not to buy more than five loaves and two fish beforehand. You may not have enough baskets to store the rest. Who can host 5000 guests? Very few. And these are guests who don't like fish and bread, at most some of them like caviar. But then there would be nothing left over. It would be impossible.

It doesn't have to make you sad. I would like to eat from the twelve baskets with the remains of the five loaves and two fish, for many reasons, also because he held it in his hand, because he broke the bread, as he did later at the Passover feast. The leftover caviar would not agree with me, would be impossible, at least that's what I keep in mind.

What if there were 1000 baskets left over? How many hungry people could be fed with it? Why were the 5000 guests so insatiable, couldn't they have left 1000 baskets?

There were enough poor people at all times, he had foreseen it. 1000 baskets, because nothing is impossible.

Very truly I tell you, whoever believes in me will do the works I have been doing, and they will do even greater things than these. (John 14:12)

8.
Biography of a tree

So you're a tree, not a bad idea. Not in the beginning. It meant being tiny, nothing more than a little dark patch of seed. What kind of tree had the biggest seeds? At least you should be such a tree at the beginning, the biggest among the small ones. Anything else is not a pleasant idea at first. You want to see the world, not grow up where your parents grew up. Not an easy thing to do. Either you let yourself be carried away as a seed by a hurricane, you could end up on rocks, in deserts or in the water. It would be the end. Or settle into a lice-ridden pelt, some animal that carries you around for free and shakes you off somewhere with other garbage. Even more pleasant than the last journey: eaten and eventually spat out at the end of a dark tube. With other garbage. Creation had arranged it strangely, the garbage was not a beauty pack, but at least it was the first growth pack.

As a sprout, you have to thrive. Fast and high. The others will not be pleased that a stranger suddenly appears in their midst, takes from their soil, light, their counted sunbeams, their water, and spreads out. You wouldn't be the first to wither away before it has even blossomed.

Eventually, the others, at odds for years, come together again, forming a dense canopy of shade, not to protect you from the heat of the sun, to deny you the air carbon dioxide to breathe. Once you've put down roots, you can't go anywhere else anyway. All paths are blocked, all roads lead towards you so that everyone can trample over you.

It makes you strong, some say, I don't know if they've been in that situation themselves.

Friends come slowly, once you've asserted yourself. Don't be too happy too soon. They want nothing more than to climb up on you, to become bigger than you, to get light in this way. Of course, they have to live off something on their way, clinging to your bark with their thousands of little claws, tapping off the delicious sap, the water, laboriously transported up from the depths by you.

And then one of them comes and starts hammering around, making holes and scars in you. At first it vibrates so nicely, like a massage, but before you know it, you're left with a nice scar and you can't defend yourself with your stiff branch arms. Not even during the storm. When the others suddenly show how flexible they are, ducking down so that the full force of the hurricane hits you.

Sometimes it is dangerous to stand stiff and upright. Others may enjoy this sublime sight, what do you gain from their joy, or do they stand in front of you when the storm comes so that you can continue to stand upright?

At some point you hear loud banging, chainsaws that mow down many of your friends like a terrible war. They're doing it for a good cause, and they call it cherishing. Don't let them cherish you, or do you want to end up as a piece of paper, printed with lies, used for something else?

Why did you become a tree anyway? Lack of an alternative? Simple but normal. 60 %. You guess? 60% of your time is spent doing things you don't like because there's no way to do what you want. Because you don't have to worry. You can stay in the same place your whole life, well protected in spite of everything, in the circle of the forest, one of thousands, not taking off, sun, air, water, getting everything delivered free without having to move.

Other reasons? Because of paradise?

Today you will be with me in paradise.

It doesn't apply to a tree, I mean today. A tree takes longer to get there. Only trees get to paradise. Because that's where the tree of life is. What a paradise, where the same thing stands everywhere. Because of the fruit? You have none of it. You work year in, year out until someone comes and takes your fruit. Because of faith? Now you're pulling my leg. Faith and belief can move mountains. I've never seen a tree move a mountain. Addiction can move mountains, the desire for a single cigarette, you wouldn't be the first to move a whole mountain of sand for it.

He told them another parable: The kingdom of heaven is like a mustard seed, which a man took and planted in his field. Though it is the smallest of all seeds, yet when it grows, it is the largest of garden plants and becomes a tree, so that the birds come and perch in its branches.
(Matthew 13:31-32)

9.
Palatial foxhole

An extremely important appointment. Certainly the most crucial in his life. A fairy tale from 1001 nights or winning the lottery. The comparisons were not enough. A license to print money, a gold mine were closer to the meaning. He had been getting ready for two hours, his wife for four hours, not that she needed it, he wanted it, it reassured him, the idea of knowing that even the last annoying little thing about his wife's facade had been brushed away, whitewashed like a potemkin.

Decision-making was sometimes not his strong point. The choice of cufflinks, he had been changing them incessantly for 20 minutes. Finally, he narrowed his eyes and decided to wear the cufflinks he had drawn at random as if from a lottery drum. Simply the plan. The idea made sense. But not examined from all sides. He drew two different ones. But what should he do? Stay true to himself, to his own decision? Who would look at both shirt sleeves at the same time? No one would notice. Risk, it still seemed more daunting to him, more terrifying than jumping without a parachute.

He had an agreement with himself. Then he was allowed to break it. Who would punish him? Himself? His larynx laughed softly. He decided on one of the two cufflinks and looked for its counterpart. Two hours, he thought. They were leaving two hours earlier, although the journey took less than forty minutes. Better safe than sorry. And there were only ten minutes left.

Ten minutes to two hours, two hours and ten minutes to the ultimate disaster, in a positive sense.

He would make a perfect bow to the President of the Republic, having practiced it with an actor, and kiss the President's wife. This kiss could be worth millions, everything had to be right, distance, temperature of the air, moisture content, just no accidental droplets of saliva, this thought made him disgusted with himself.

We'll be leaving in ten minutes, he called to his wife in the next room.

She didn't respond. He threw on his tails and went next door. She was standing almost naked in front of the mirror. He didn't know which reaction was the most appropriate. An explosion, a storm, a thunderstorm with gale-force winds? He broke off at the last moment. Beauty comes from within, he thought. Not the right moment for drama, it would upset his wife, and the four-hour masquerade would be washed away in the storm of his words.

Do you need help? he asked. His irritable mood could not be heard.

I'll be ready in a minute, she said.
And managed it. They left on time. Oscar winners appeared no less dressed up for the awards ceremony. The sun faded in its brilliance. And retreated in shame behind thick clouds. They arrived far too early. Waited. Sitting in the car for over an hour. They didn't say a word. They were silent for an hour. With themselves, with their environment, with their thoughts, with their thinking. There was nothing around them, black emptiness filled with dynamite dust, one wrong word and everything would blow up, explode.
Then the time had come. He started the engine and they drove the last little distance. The gate was locked. At the end of an endless gravel path, they recognized the foothills of the estate. He

hadn't expected it to be so far away. If they weren't allowed to drive up, they wouldn't make it in time on foot. Sweat trickled down his forehead. To be late. Unthinkable. One second. It would be a catastrophe, the expected great earthquake in California, unceremoniously happening in his lifetime, in a fraction of an instant. The opportunities, money-printing machine, carefree life, goldmine, blown away in an instant.

Lost in thought, he didn't notice the porter standing next to the car. He had come out of his little house next to the wrought-iron gate. He turned the windows in a negative direction, the fresh evening air was good.

Mr. Bernardino, I presume?

He nodded. He couldn't get a word out. His insides were no longer moistly mirroring, they were dried up, a speechless desert.

I am to give you this letter, Mr. Bernardino. The President apologizes. He deeply regrets it.

He took the letter with trembling hands. The doorman would not budge. He remained standing by the car.

Mr. Bernardino, the President wants you to read the letter immediately.

Immediately, he repeated. There was uncertainty in his voice, his whole body was full of it.

After two minutes, his dark face brightened. Satisfied waves of a smile rolled across the wrinkles on his face.

Now tell me what it says, his wife prodded.

He, he, he has appointed me secretary of state, not just any city clerk. I'm going to be in charge of his office.

And Mr. Bernardino, may I inform the president that you accept? The doorman had made his presence felt once more.

Tell him it is an honor for me, a gracious honor, to put myself, my life, my soul, at his service. I will do my best.

The doorman had expected this answer. He reached into his pocket and pulled a key into the evening light.

For your official villa. From now on, you will live at 1 Upper Street.

1 Upper Street, he repeated incredulously. Everyone knew the property. At least 30 rooms, 15 bathrooms, a huge dining room, old-style men's rooms, several lounges, a library, fitness rooms in the basement, a swimming pool, a sauna

and a covered tennis court behind the house on the huge grounds.

He finally knew why he had always been one hundred percent loyal. It paid off to have been a supporter of the President back then. In retrospect, the house alone justified his subservience, not a house, not a villa, but rather an estate, palatial, twenty houses, at least twenty normal houses could be packed into this palace and there would still be enough room to lay his head.

Foxes have dens and birds have nests, but the Son of Man has no place to lay his head.
(Matthew 8:20)

10.
Dinner tie

We should order four more places.

Four places, isn't that too expensive?

A bit. But I remembered too late that we forgot the Yellstones and Myers.

Yellstones, they never invited us.

You're right. But their parents often invited my parents. I spent a lot of time at their place as a child. Last month I found my father's diary.

You found your father's diary? Why didn't you tell me about it?

Sorry, I forgot. Here, look: 16:15.

Was your father a football player?

No. 16:15 for the Yellstones. I kept a tally as I was reading. Yellstones invited us 16 times, we only invited them 15 times. My father had another dinner planned. He died suddenly.

Yes, I know. And now you mean...

Exactly, they are still owed another invitation. Then it's even. Back in balance.

Well, if you say so.

I think it's right. We can't put it on the kids. Tomorrow I'll call the restaurant and order four extra places.

Good. I mean with Yellstones. But why the Myers. We've never been to visit them.

The Myers are important. He works at Hapoylo Company. I'll be ready to apply there in two years.

I see.

Yes, I don't know exactly what position Myers holds. With a bit of luck, we'll get talking. Next time at the latest.

What do you mean?

I'll invite Myers today, then he'll have to invite me too. It's quite simple, isn't it? Another connection forged. For our safety net. We can't fall anymore.

All right, four extra places. That's okay.

Another thought occurred to me.

Don't make it so suspenseful.

At the last invitation at Richetson's, remember?

No, there were too many appointments.

Richetsons have this big house with a huge swimming pool in the garden.

Yes, I know.

They had set up a small pontoon stage in the middle for a few musicians. Music straight from the water.

Oh yes, I'd forgotten. It was a great atmosphere.

And the dance floor all around. The dance on the water volcano.

Great idea.

Everyone was amazed.

We can't keep up with that. Maybe in two or three years, when you start at Hapoylo and we can afford a bigger house.

We don't have to do the same thing. It would be in bad taste.

What are you going to do?

I told you earlier about Richie, my best friend from school. He works as a performance artist in Las Vegas. Own show. Made it big. I've already spoken to him. He'd do a show for free. We'd only have to pay the hall rental for an additional room in the restaurant and the transportation costs.

Transportation costs?

He works with white tigers. He takes care of the authorization from the authorities himself. Would like to see the faces of the Richetsons when we drive up the white tigers.

How much does it cost?

We'll have to take out a small loan. It's worth it. Think of Hapoylo Company. Myers will extend us a return invitation. I mentioned in passing that I'm interested in a career change. If I start working for Hapoylo, we can pay off the loan with no problem.

What can I say? You need to know what's right. Do you actually have Millers on the guest list?

Millers, no.

Why not?

We no longer have an open invitation with them. In fact, I think we've had them over more often than the other way around.

Millers could do with it.

Why?

He is out of work. And they gambled, on the stock market, you know?

You mean Millers are broke?

As far as I know, yes.

That's a shame. Twice as bad.

Why twice?

They don't fit into the circle. Think about it. Myers happens to be talking to Miller. Well, how are you, what do you do for a living, how many hundreds of thousands of dollars do you earn a year, just the usual blah blah blah. And Miller can only answer: Not good, I'm not doing well, no job, no more assets, just sold the house. Myers must be thinking, but we have some strange people in our circle of acquaintances.

Do you actually know what you're talking about?

Pretty much. Let's invite the Millers to a private party. Just them and us, small group. You make a few pizzas, and we'll have a little chat. That's all we can afford for others at the moment anyway. The loan for the tigers. The hall hire. Do you understand?

We can wait until the Millers are homeless. Talk to them on the park bench, take them to a fast food restaurant and feed them there. It'll be even cheaper, she concluded caustically.

When you give a luncheon or dinner, do not invite your friends, your brothers or sisters, your relatives, or your rich neighbors; if you do, they may invite you back and so you will be repaid. But when you give a banquet, invite the poor, the crippled, the lame, the blind, and you will be blessed. Although they cannot repay you, you will be repaid at the resurrection of the righteous. (Luke 14:12-14)

11.
Constructed ruin

We can never make it good. You can't turn bad into good. Turning a spoiled sausage into a tasty one is impossible, at best through deception, fraud, the spoiled part remains in the product, even if it has become unrecognizable. Our task is not to make amends. The fathers are to blame. Should we pay for it?

Thoughts came to his mind that he had not called for. The main task was to help the survivors of terror. To compensate for the damage as far as possible. Once the survivors had left this earth, didn't this responsibility cease? Only in part. Didn't the responsibility remain to ensure that something similar would never happen again? That was the second part of the responsibility to oneself, to one's own children, to the victims anyway.

A building was planned for this. A memorial. A memorial for all time. Visible from afar, audible even further, unmistakable, whether anyone wanted it or not. Weeks, months, years passed, passed from the idea to the vision, from the vision to the agreement on a common denominator, from the agreement on a common denominator to the planning, from the planning to the choice of a company, it was to be immaculate, like snow on the summit of the highest mountain, untouched by guilt. In the terrible confusion, the head of state finally intervened with clear words to fill in the gaps, untangle the confusion and turn ideas into reality.

They realized their mistake too late. In none of the steps had they — yes, they had really forgotten — it was unbelievable, it had never occurred to anyone. Nor would it have occurred to them if one day an old man had not asked to see the President.

It was an election year and the President thought it was a good idea to pay attention to the elderly. In his enormous office, he sat behind a desk the size of which had swallowed up at least ten giant jungle trees. The President was enthroned on the sunny side, his chair raised several centimeters. The old man crouched opposite, his voice brittle with the breath of terrible decades.

I was there, the old man said in a low voice.

He didn't get an answer, not for a while. The situation made his conversation partner uncomfortable.

You don't need to give me much time, the old man continued. I will show you something. But a few moments of your time.

The President felt compelled to go on the offensive. He pulled open a desk drawer and unrolled a huge drawing. He studied the other man's eyes attentively.

How do you like that, if you can even speak of liking in this context?

Now the old man fell silent. His eyes, which had receded far back, remained fixed. In front of him was the image of a huge building, surrounded by countless monuments, an oppressive past cast in stone, the sight of which would never disappear from our minds.

We will build this, said the President. As a memorial for all the victims, for them and the others. Millions, we need space for millions of names.

The old man stood up. He placed a box on the desk and raised his brittle voice one last time.

Think it over again. You don't need to build your huge facility. This is enough.

He left the room in silence. Months passed, the construction work had begun, a huge pit like an oversized grave had been dug, to anchor the foundations in the body of the earth. Weeks went by. Several construction companies had filed for bankruptcy in the meantime. There were constant disputes with the architect. One debate followed another about the escalating costs.

One evening, the President was sitting in his office when his eyes fell on the small box. He had placed it in a remote corner of his study. When he opened it, he was met by a small sculpture. A tree, not green, although the surroundings revealed summer, with a small child sitting beneath it. Only once did he look at the sculpture's face, the fine features, not yet worn by age, yet the expression of a face that had already seen all the suffering in the world. He would never forget that expression. There was a torn note in the box, the paper old, written on by a child's hand:

I have lived underground. And yet the sun was shining.

The construction project was well advanced, but it could no longer be saved. Construction companies, architects and politicians were all at loggerheads. The most serious problem was the lack of money. Politically, it was not possible to mobilize more money in this time of crisis. As a result, the huge complex remained a ruin, and many people walked past it in amazement. Everything had been planned, the size, the costs, the materials, doors, windows, and now they had to leave everything unfinished in the middle of it all.

Suppose one of you wants to build a tower. Won't you first sit down and estimate the cost to see if you have enough money to complete it? For if you lay the foundation and are not able to finish it, everyone who sees it will ridicule you, saying, This person began to build and wasn't able to finish. (Luke 14:28-30)

12.
Blind guides

John Smith took a deep breath. His first vacation in ten years. Ten years of work, hard, relentless, karate-chopping resistance, outwitting opponents, wrapping banks around his finger. Ten exciting, ten miserable, ten normal years of life.

The company was finally running, it was on the right track, uphill, and it ran itself. Where did such a thing exist? A train that ran uphill without any drive. After ten years. Take a deep breath, right down to the last alveolus, soak up the heaviness of the last few years and blow it away with relish into the shimmering heat of the African steppe. Here he stood, a big game hunter who had killed his first trophy, struck down by him, a monster in the shape of ten years. Better than a shot lion, a conquered tiger, he had killed the most difficult thing, his past.

Tomorrow he will see a gamekeeper, and together they will go on safari for two weeks. He knew his way around the urban jungle. His business: unusual sightseeing tours, off the beaten track, crossing slums, roaming port districts, chirping through red light districts, hitting unusual bars – no problem for him.

He looked at the steppe through binoculars. Suddenly, a lion appeared in his field of vision. Large, majestic, footsteps in slow motion, he was startled, footsteps heading straight for him. He pulled down the binoculars and hurried to the car. The animal also quickened its steps, he couldn't see it, he had his back turned towards it.

Idiot, he thought to himself, why are you driving into the wilderness alone on the first day? There are no mafia bosses running around here, no pimps, no freaked-out types, no violent criminals, he was in the heart of real danger, a blind man in the black night, even though the sun was beating down on his shaven head.

After falling into the car, he hammered wildly on the lock. As if a lion could open the door. The big cat had stopped anyway. It had probably realized the futility of the undertaking. Besides, a fattening big city two-legged creature, nothing but a snack at a dirty slum snack bar, compared to the five-star menu of a young gazelle.

The lion turned away, perhaps it just wanted to have a bit of fun, show who was master of the house, boss of the steppe.

John Smith started the car, his hands still shaking. With screeching tires, he drove off, not away, heading straight for the lion. The animal did not move. It remained motionless for a long while. The speed of the jeep increased inexorably. Only now did the wildcat turn and chase across the steppe. John Smith rubbed his eyes in amazement. The lion was not fleeing, it was heading straight for him. He had read about a lioness that had adopted a gazelle. Crazy animal. But not fighting a jeep.

John Smith slammed on the brakes, mightily, a sledgehammer, the car roared and began to skid. Smith was thrown forward. His head touched the windshield, his eyes forward, through the glass, staring directly into the lion's eyes. Then the animal was gone – with a mighty leap over the car, leaving a wet scent mark in the air as a sign of victory, he saw in the rear-view mirror how the lion slowly dissolved into the cover of the wilderness.

John Smith was nothing but a blind man, he needed the best gamekeeper, that much was certain. He fixed it. The next day. In the capital. He simply let his instincts guide him and ran straight to the first office, on the door of which he found a sign for safari tours.

The man was barely older than him, his skin cooked through, crispy, brown, with straw hair on top and a deep, whisky-soaked voice. Not necessarily likeable, but that wasn't the point. John Smith needed him to savor every second of his vacation by turning the African veldt upside down. They quickly came to an agreement. The price for ten days was reasonable, including equipment and off-road vehicle. The departure was to take place in two days so that John Smith could acclimatize sufficiently by then.

Then the time had finally come.

They raced across the dry grass at 80 km/h, sowing thick clouds of dust, with startled animals crawling out of every conceivable corner and fleeing. They chased through the terrain for two days. John Smith had bought himself the shooting of a lion.

Bryan, it was the name of the safari guide, was surprised at his strange customer. Almost every hour they got a magnificent animal in front of the shotgun. John Smith never pulled the trigger. He waited. For the lion that had duped him days ago. The eyes. He would recognize them immediately. And then pull the trigger. A shot between the eyes, at the same moment the animal dared to jump over his car a second time. On the third day, they spotted the animal. Rather by chance. They had set off a little earlier and passed a watering hole. The big cat was resting in the shade of a tree. It was familiar with the sound of the engine and made no attempt to flee. It was only when John Smith raised his rifle that the lion jumped up and – unexpectedly – did not charge towards the car but fled.

John Smith stood upright and took aim at the fleeing animal. Bryan got the last out of the off-road vehicle. The vegetation became denser, and the silhouette of the lion appeared less and less frequently in the bush grass.

Suddenly there was a huge bang. The car had plunged unchecked into a pit teeming with snakes and scorpions. It took some time for the men to recover from their fright.

John Smith was the first to speak:

I thought you knew the area like the back of your hand, he said angrily.

The safari guide looked at him with wide eyes, fear, terror, anxiety, everything reflected in his gaze.

I think I have something to confess to you, he said in a trembling voice. It's my first tour.

It's what? John Smith shouted.

My first tour. I'm actually a machinist. Been out of work for a month. You've got to do something.

John Smith looked up the walls of the pit from below. He thought he was in the hands of the best gamekeeper and found himself in a dark snake pit. The pit, the end of his vacation, the first in ten years, buried in a pit.

Leave them; they are blind guides. If the blind lead the blind, both will fall into a pit.
(Matthew 15:14)

13.
Shiny appearance

The war was over. An unwanted visitor who had finally moved on. Overdue. His departure. There was hardly anything left to pick up anyway. Rubble and ash mostly, no water to wash it away, all the crushed dirt, a nasty puddle that had spread everywhere. A jug of water. A jug a day. For one family. That was all that was allotted.

In the lakes and rivers, in ponds and streams, rotting corpses everywhere, spewed out by the overeating war. They were castaways of time, water everywhere, the past, yet they were dying of thirst.

A jug of water. Here the choice remained, what to use it for? To drink? The body could thirst and extract the water from the meagre food. For washing? Who did you want to be beautiful for? The dead no longer look at you. To brush your teeth? Questions after questions.

He had built up a little business of his own. People had to drink. Not water. Alcohol. What was still left had to be preserved. Water was much more difficult to organize than alcohol. At one point, he thought about distilling water out of alcohol. In the end, it was too laborious.

Slowly the demand grew. In the beginning. As long as his senses were clear. Which meant nothing else: the glasses had to be cleaner. Otherwise, the customers would stay away. Times changed, the distance to the war was greater, the demands grew with the distance, almost exponentially. There was even lipstick again, he found the traces on the rim of the glasses.

Only water remained scarce. He traded. Water for cigarettes, water for all sorts of things. He earned much more from the full glasses. But they had to be clean.

He thought about it. The surface area of the glasses was smaller on the inside than on the outside. It made sense to only clean the inside. It was also more important. What difference did it make if there was dirt on the outside? Of course it mattered, a lot, even a great deal.

People wouldn't come back. Drinking from dirty glasses – nobody needed it anymore. Besides, alcohol disinfected. The bacteria, the dirt inside the glass, it didn't matter, the alcohol would put an end to everything. And the glasses were frosted, tinted, the inside surface wasn't translucent, people could see the dirt on the outside, but not on the inside, what wasn't visible didn't exist.

That's why he only washed the outside of the glasses, it saved water, almost half, and people came in droves, attracted by the alcohol, attracted by the outer shine of the glasses.

Woe to you, teachers of the law and Pharisees, you hypocrites! You clean the outside of the cup and dish, but inside they are full of greed and self-indulgence. Blind Pharisee! First clean the inside of the cup and dish, and then the outside also will be clean. (Matthew 23:25-26)

14.

The trembling emptiness

A wave, powerful, deep vibrations, straight from the bowels of the earth. No sooner had it appeared in the dawning daylight than it rolled across the ground, towards the beach, where the water rose and fell restlessly. The unimaginable mountains of waves crushed everything in their path. Small flat houses, crouched in hollows, then nothing more than a narrow sheet of paper. Many had already gone to bed, others were sitting down to dinner, others were lying together. The shock wave raced over everything, pressing bodies lying on top of each other into each other, shattering sleeping, peaceful dreams, sweeping away confused lives and leaving the old bodies lifeless.

Shortly afterwards, the ocean spilled over the city in a kilometer-high fountain, for a moment the ocean basin was completely empty, all the water piled over the city, not even a fraction of a second and it was over.

The destroyed houses were washed away, dead, injured, sick life, young and old, swept away by the flood. Stripped bare, the patch of earth lay before the mountain range, just like the day before creation, untouched, shaped by the elemental force of destruction, waiting for what came next.

See to it that you are not alarmed. There will be earthquakes in various places.
(Matthew 24:7)

The miserable bleating of the thirsty animals could be heard from afar, a plea to the clouds, which were somewhere behind this endless glowing blue, to pour down some of their precious water. In vain. Nothing stirred in the firmament. Not even a cool breeze moved across the land.
The woman had crawled into the farthest corner of the cave. Her body was mostly bare, and she was leaning large parts of her naked skin against the cool, damp walls of the cave, trying to transfer some of its freshness to her body. Days ago, her eyes had been wide, fish eyes, to find a scrap of edible food lying around. In vain. So her pupils had narrowed and her eyes had crept far into their own sockets.
Her stomach ached, she could feel her stomach eating steadily, incessantly from the inside outwards. Soon it would stick its grimace

outside, go in search of food itself. She used a sharp stone to inflict injuries on her arm, to cover the pain of her guts. Any pain seemed more bearable than the furious stinging of her guts, which had been starving and thirsting for days.

Her senses were becoming increasingly clouded. The entrance to the cave opened and plants, magnificently adorned with plump, red fruit, moved towards her on two legs. They bowed low before her, she only had to stretch out her arms, raise her hand, she lacked the strength, she couldn't move a millimeter, any part of her body.

The plants screwed up their faces in astonishment, turned around and left the cave again. What was that? A miracle. One of the strange guests had left a piece of bread behind. The mild brown color of the baked cereal soothed her insides. She felt strength rising within her, slowly, but surely more and more. Life came back into her body from above. Her lips moved, pools of saliva gathered in her mouth, her arms rose, her whole body was suddenly gripped by a violent storm and she threw herself forward on to the abandoned piece of bread.

The first greeting of life in how many days. How many days, how many weeks, she didn't know. Carefully she put her parched lips over the crust, the outside was hard, then she pressed her teeth into it with all her might to tear out a piece of life from her prey. For minutes she chewed on the tree bark, close to madness, her mind, the cracked lips, the piercing pain, no part of her body wanted to admit it. She least of all.

See to it that you are not alarmed. There will be famines in various places.
(Matthew 24:7)

15.

Cold hated love

Then many will fall and hate and betray each other. And in many, love will grow cold.

The room was a reflection of his imagination. Four walls, no window, a plain desk, two chairs, one on each side of the table, a third in the corner.

Take a seat.

He took a seat, already in the process of resting his elongated spine on the bare wooden chair.

Do you know what your statement means?

The person addressed remained silent.

Well, let's start with the end. Here's a sheet of paper. Blank, as you can see. Put your name underneath.

My name? I don't know what I'm signing.

Don't you trust us? The man's voice became sharper.

Of course I do. It's simply. My upbringing. You understand. Don't sign anything you haven't read. My parents. You do understand. They were good people, devoted to their country. They passed it on to me.

Your parents didn't know us. They would have told you that they could trust us more blindly than anything.

When he had written his name, the officer pulled back the paper and looked at the letters.

Beautiful handwriting. You must have had really good parents. Order, manners, discipline, it's reflected in your letters.

He smiled sheepishly.

So, your name is Peter Nuntius, the officer continued. Well, Mr. Nuntius. We must make haste. You're not the only one who wants to make a statement. 30 are still waiting. Just for me. Our department has 20 officers. 20 × 30, do you understand? 600 statements from people about people. Hard work, less for them than for us.

He remained silent and so the officer took the opportunity to ask another question.

Are you related to this Schrebenecz?

What are you thinking? Peter Nuntius defended himself resolutely. With an object like that!

It doesn't matter, interrupted the officer. You wouldn't believe how many people make statements about relatives. I keep a little statistic about it. 50%, at least 50%, come because of their relatives. Let's leave that alone. Just tell me what you know.

Nuntius took a breath, deep, very deep, he drew the words out of his guts. They rattled like a rusty anchor chain over his tongue, moved back and forth by shaky waves.

I'll make it short, Nuntius finally said and reached deep into his pocket. Here. The note. This Schreberecz put it in my letterbox. Secretly. Thought I wouldn't notice.

The officer looked at the crumpled paper. Then he let out a low whistle.

Good work, Nuntius, he said approvingly. The first useful lead from these groups. Schrebenecz is one of them. He will lead us to the others.

My reward, stuttered Nuntius, I mean, is there anything for it.

The officer beckoned the assistant to come over. The man disappeared for a moment and returned with a leather box. It contained a medal.

It's more than money, the officer noted. Walk the streets with it during the day, you'll find it confirmed.

He addressed one last question to Nuntius:

Do you actually know this Schrebenecz?

Nuntius nodded.

We are old schoolmates. There's no discrepancy with what I said earlier.

And you know what will happen to him?

Yes, Nuntius replied. But I can't take that into consideration.

You are a splendid man, the officer concluded the conversation. Your heart is in the right place. You set your priorities as they should be.

Nuntius pinned the medal to his lapel, clearly visible to all. The officer paid no more attention to him. He made a note in his diary and phoned the security service. It wouldn't be an hour before this Schrebenecz would be kneeling before him, whimpering and moaning. No matter. He also knew how to prioritize.

See to it that you are not alarmed. Many will turn away from the faith and will betray and hate each other. The love of most will grow cold. (Matthew 24:6,10,12).

16.
Two-sided parallel weddings

The band had played themselves into a frenzy. Faster and faster the bows flew over the strings, the wind players blasted oblique air into their instruments, all driven by the drums that drove the music forward like a storm. The dance floor was overflowing. Countless legs swayed across the floor, electrified by the music, fighting against the swaying rhythm of the copious amounts of wine.

What a party. The exuberance knew no bounds. Beaming, laughing, jubilant faces, red, chubby-cheeked, glowing eyes, sweat-soaked shirts. It was undoubtedly the high point in the history of the village, there had not been a similar celebration in living memory and a comparable one would not come again for a long time. Who knows, perhaps it was the most exhilarating wedding the country had seen.

30 lambs slaughtered, the aromas wafting from huge silver dishes, carved oxen and pigs, suckling pigs beyond counting, mountains of bread, fruit, great piles of cheese and whole lakes filled with heavy, sweet wine. What a feast. Between the

dances, the guests rushed to the tables, stuffed themselves with the delicacies and washed them down with a good measure of liquid. Then back to the dance floor. With other partners, now and then tightly embraced, eyes burning into each other.

Suddenly the music stopped. It was agreed. Silence for a moment, not a sound, not a grin, not a smacking of the lips, not a swallow, not a single word. The first musician began to stamp his feet on the floor. Another followed. The third joined in, a chain, until all the musicians were stepping to the same rhythm. Now those present began to understand and stamped their feet to the same beat, on the same floor, as if they wanted to kick through the ceiling. The first instrument sounded, delicate, sweet, an endlessly distant nightingale approaching the deafening rhythm. The concert master caught the delicate melody and transfigured it into heavenly spheres with his violin. The wind instruments were silent, only the violins joined in, one after the other.

Underneath, the hard rhythm of the legs thundered. The volume of the music swelled, taking up the fight against the powerful rhythm, yet losing none of its sweetness. The feet stomped faster, and the sweet violin sounds floated through the hall. Both increased, faster, louder, louder, faster, louder, louder, faster, one could not catch up with the other, the polka steamed through the room and swept everyone along with it.

It was the moment for the bride's entrance. Carried by the sounds of the violin, the woman in white floated through the stamping bodies and suddenly stood in the middle of the hall. There had never been a more beautiful woman. Her shining green eyes stood out through the white veil, waves of thick black hair spilled over her back, her finely chiseled body stood out in wondrously delicate curves from the silhouette of the bridal gown. The man's eyes were so bulging that the fish had to fear for their uniqueness.

The bridegroom appeared, and now the women came into their own. He towered over their aged, fat husbands by the length of their heads, his shiny hair flowed without a transition onto the black silk tailcoat, his perfectly developed muscles stood out through the supple silk, as if one could see his body stripped of all material. The pounding of the legs regained the upper hand and pushed back the sweet sounds of the violin.

Carried by the music, the bride hovered above the floor like a hummingbird and the groom moved towards the white figure to the rhythm of the stomping polka. The rhythm of the music was transferred to the floor. Walls began to vibrate, dishes rattled, first softly, then louder and louder, the dead lambs began to move again in the vibrations of the vibrating room, the suckling pigs squealed and a muffled roar came from the roasting oxen.

Then the floor collapsed and pulled everyone down with it.

But about that day or hour no one knows, not even the angels in heaven, nor the Son, but only the Father. As it was in the days of Noah, so it will be at the coming of the Son of Man. For in the days before the flood, people were eating and drinking, marrying and giving in marriage, up to the day Noah entered the ark; and they knew nothing about what would happen until the flood came and took them all away. That is how it will be at the coming of the Son of Man.
(Matthew 24:37-39)

Index

Biography

After graduating from high school in Berlin, I studied medicine in Berlin and Munich and worked in medicine for around 40 years after my studies. I have been retired since the end of 2022. During my professional career I also wrote some manuscripts, a book for young people, children's books, novels and poems. Some have since been self-published.

In addition the author has published several novels in English translation:

Manu's Journey With Death
- A fugue through time

A life, narrated on several levels, accompanied in its tracks and followed by death. In some places, points of this life that have long since passed light up, a brief glowing breath where it pauses for a moment before it is dragged on by the stream of life and disappears somewhere, not without trace but forever. What remains? In any case, death, even if no one is interested in the remnants of this trace of life.

Chrystillian Christmas –
Christmas as usual ~~and~~ different

A goose on its flight to baking-oven land, chasing a golden angel's curl, encountering a mutant Christmas tree, an endless line of waiting stars, Santa's great-great-ancestor and, of course, Father Christmas himself, sitting on a cloud under whose shadow a boy is riding down from the peaks of the Andes, spreading the news of Christ's birth ... It could be like that, but it isn't quite, maybe a little, but just maybe. An Advent calendar of Christmas short stories, profound and loving, varied and multi-faceted, presented in a wonderful narrative style that will enchant even the adult reader. A fragrance-wrapped Christmas soufflé that can be eaten over 26+1 days, on each day of Advent and Christmas plus New Year's Eve, or all at once, depending on the size of your appetite or Christmas taste ...

The Island of Figures
Youth Novel

A little girl in Japan receives a doll from her father for her birthday. When the girl is older, the doll is placed on the waves of the sea in a small boat. Apparently a tradition to mark the transition to a new phase of life into adulthood.

Some time later, another girl travels after her missing doll, and an exciting, adventurous journey begins with an unusual, surprising end.

Roxanna
And the Mysterious Monk

Detective Roxanna has solved her first case when life, or rather death, puts another case on her desk. This brings her into contact with a wealthy English gentleman at his country estate, who has amassed a considerable fortune with an unusual business idea. Among them is a complicated hunter, who is not only a little over-the-top in his language, and especially a monk who, with his incredible intuition, not only beats the inspector to it once.

Roxanna

The Fatal Secret of the Murder Books

It begins with a murder, a somewhat bizarre female detective, events that take place in Rome, England and France. A story that jumps back to the Middle Ages, runs on two tracks, two suspicious women and a dead man who suddenly appears one night to one of the two suspects. A tangled criminal string that seems to have been partially untangled by diligent endeavours — only to become even more tangled in the next moment and finally, seemingly lying in front of you untangled in a perfectly straight line.

Allegories

Short Stories Volume 1 -4

The following collection in 4 volumes contains just over 60 short stories, each short story is based on a biblical passage from the New Testament like a parable and is applied to our time. A short time to catch your breath, a short time perhaps to reflect, a short time perhaps to delve deeper. Although Christ used everyday life for his parables, they still leave a deep impression today. They are easy to remember with a hidden important message that we discover when we think about them.

Uhlenspiegel with the Schilda Citizens

Uhlenspiegel, the lone warrior, armed with an army of mischievous thoughts, encounters a village full of Schilda citizens who are less armed, or rather, armed with different thoughts. Uhlenspiegel's premise: "Where money is at stake, it's good to be good!" And so he mischievously plays out his insights on the Schilda citizens who, with their naive way of thinking, are the appropriate antagonists. Does such an encounter make sense? Amusing and entertaining, in any case!